Published by TapestryPublishing.com

ISBN 978-0-692865-02-6

Based on the original poem "Suppose."

©2013 Expressions of Life   **www.paulsamuels.com**

Original illustrations conceptualized by Bob Trochim and
illustrated by Linn Winsted Trochim.

Printed and bound in the United States of America.

———————————

Dedicated to my wife of 41 years: Arlene Bridges Samuels,
our son Chad Bridges Samuels and daughter Gloria Grace Samuels.

You inspire me each day with your love and support!

Many thanks to my wonderful illustrator Linn Trochim,
Animart_Adelphia1@comcast.net, who literally gave life to
my characters.

And thanks to Debbie Decker for the professional
page layout, editing and cover designs.

From a young boy's face I snitched a nose...

1

... and stuck it down between my toes!

2

Now what do you suppose you would do if the
nose between my toes belonged to you?

Would you laugh or would you cry?

Or would you simply try to get by without a nose upon your face and live your life in total disgrace?

From a girl's face I plucked a smile and hid it down the road a mile.

What do you suppose you would do if the smile I plucked belonged to you?

You couldn't laugh without first having a smile, so you'd be thinking sad thoughts for quite a while.

But maybe the postman will come by and put a
smile in your eye and on your face when you see
your smile's hiding place.

8

From another boy's head I took an ear and
hid it away for about a year.

9

And what do you suppose you would do if the ear I took belonged to you?

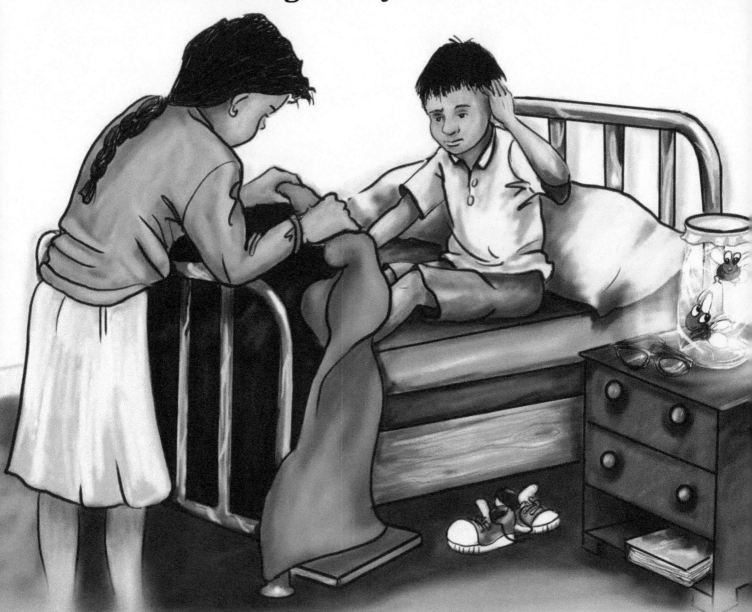

Would you hold your hand against your head and not take it down until you went to bed?

10

You couldn't wear glasses because they'd slide off your face, and you'd look awfully silly running in a race!

11

The year is over and I'm sure you're glad
your ear is back—you're no longer sad.

From another girl I plucked two eyes and
hid them away in some apple pies.

Now what do you suppose you would do if
the eyes in the pies belonged to you?

You couldn't look around because you couldn't see, so you'd never be able to know it was me.

15

But you might one day eat some apple pies
and inside a pie just may find your eyes.

Then from a boy and a girl I grabbed one mouth each and hid them in a sandcastle on the beach.

What do you suppose you would do if the mouth in the sandcastle belonged to you?

You'd have to get there before high tide, or your mouth would float away far and wide!

19

And you couldn't even say a word or sound,
unless on the beach your mouth you found.

But you have a nose and you have a smile, and
I love when you flash it every once in a while.

You have your eyes and your cute little ears,
and you've had them all for a number of years.

You have your mouth to complete your God-given face; no matter what you look like, you are no disgrace.

Yes, the face you have belongs only to you, and here's what you're SUPPOSED to do:

LIKE yourself and BELIEVE God loves you, then you can tell others that He loves them, too!

"Suppose"

A Poem about Liking Yourself

From a young boy's face I snitched a nose… and stuck it down between my toes!
Now what do you suppose you would do if the nose between my toes belonged to you?
Would you laugh or would you cry? Or would you simply try to get by
    without a nose upon your face and live your life in total disgrace?

From a girl's face I plucked a smile and hid it down the road a mile.
What do you suppose you would do if the smile I plucked belonged to you?
You couldn't laugh without first having a smile,
    so you'd be thinking sad thoughts for quite a while.
But maybe the postman will come by and put a smile in your eye
    and on your face when you see your smile's hiding place.

From another boy's head I took an ear and hid it away for about a year.
And what do you suppose you would do if the ear I took belonged to you?
Would you hold your hand against your head and not take it down until you went to bed?
You couldn't wear glasses because they'd slide off your face,
    and you'd look awfully silly running in a race!
The year is over and I'm sure you're glad your ear is back—you're no longer sad.

From another girl I plucked two eyes and hid them away in some apple pies.
Now what do you suppose you would do if the eyes in the pies belonged to you?
You couldn't look around because you couldn't see, so you'd never be able to know it was me.
But you might one day eat some apple pies and inside the pies just may find your eyes.

Then from a boy and a girl I grabbed one mouth each and hid them in a sandcastle on the beach.
What do you suppose you would do if the mouth in the sandcastle belonged to you?
You'd have to get there before high tide, or your mouth would float away far and wide!
And you couldn't even say a word or sound, unless on the beach your mouth you found.

But you have a nose and you have a smile, and I love when you flash it every once in a while.
You have your eyes and your cute little ears, and you've had them all for a number of years.
You have your mouth to complete your God-given face;
    no matter what you look like, you are no disgrace.
Yes, the face you have belongs only to you, and here's what you're SUPPOSED to do:
LIKE yourself and BELIEVE God loves you, then you can tell others that He loves them, too!

In his professional ministry career, Paul served in senior positions with World Vision, Mercy Ships, Youth with a Mission and the Messianic Jewish Alliance of America. He is married to Arlene Bridges Samuels, a former Miss Florence, South Carolina. Paul and Arlene have two adult children: Chad Bridges Samuels and Gloria Grace Samuels.

Suppose is Paul's third book. It opens a door for young children to explore the possibility of liking themselves the way Jesus taught. Paul's first book titled *Where is Christmas?* is a delightful woodland journey that leads children from preschool to fourth grade to discover the real Christmas. He also authored an inspirational, contemporary book of poetry entitled *Expressions of Life* along with 91 Retro Greeting Cards formerly sold in college and Bible bookstores (now available at **www.zazzle.com/retrogreetingcards/products**).

Linn Winsted Trochim began her career in the film-animation industry in Hollywood, California, drawing famous characters such as The Flintstones® and Scooby Doo® for Hanna-Barbera Studios. Linn and her late husband Bob opened Animart Studios in Colorado Springs, Colorado to produce animation for television and computers. Linn later focused her talent on illustrating multiple forms of media, where she discovered her true passion: creating children's art. Linn also illustrated Paul's book *Where is Christmas?* with Bob. She can be reached at **Animart_Adelphia1@comcast.net**.

Other books by Paul L. Samuels are available at **www.TapestryPublishing.com**:

Woody Squirrel and friends discover the truth about Christmas!

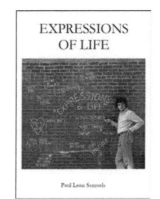

A journey of the emotions through poetry

"Suppose you are a child who imagines life as no one else imagines. Suppose you believe you are different from everyone else. Suppose you don't know WHAT to think about it. Then this book is for you!

Paul Samuels captures the imagination and heart of a child with his prose and empathy while artist Linn Trochim brings Paul's thoughts to life through her illustrations. *Suppose* transports children to an imaginary existence that validates and encourages their unique and beautiful identity. Children will be captivated by the story as they see themselves on each page while being drawn into the brilliant scenes. This book was written not just to be read but also experienced."

Ray Snyder, Professor of Business, Trident Technical College, Charleston, SC
and author of *The Business of Families*

***

"Paul Samuels' creative mind spills over in a way that makes me wish I were a child again just to have someone read the story to me. This book awakens the mind of a child to see and understand things that other media might bury."

Gayle D. Erwin, author-of *The Jesus Style*

***

Suppose is a playful, imaginative work from Paul Samuels that will certainly pique the curiosity of children. His lyrical expressions will make kids smile and laugh as they consider the silly situations he describes. Best of all, the story he weaves provides readers with an important truth on which to build their lives.

Over the years I have invited Paul as a guest speaker for children and adults alike. I can already imagine him delighting audiences as he dramatizes each situation and look forward to seeing *Suppose* in libraries and classrooms everywhere.

Cindy Hunnicutt, Family Pastor, Restoration Church, Alpharetta, GA

CPSIA information can be obtained
at www.ICGtesting.com
Printed in the USA
BVHW02*1504040918
526426BV00006BA/9/P

9 780692 865026